Sally

by Leslie Carr

HOUGHTON MIFFLIN

BOSTON

Key Vocabulary

biography the story of a person's life, told by another person

facts things that are true

events things that happen

sequence when one thing follows another in order

research the careful study of something

Word Teaser

When you do this vocabulary word you search for information. What is it?

Sally Ride was the first American woman to travel into space. Her biography tells about the things that happened in her life.

A tennis player

Sally Ride was born in California in 1951. One of the important facts about her early life is that she loved to play tennis. At first she wanted to be a tennis star.

A woman scientist

But, after three months, Sally changed her mind. She went to college and decided that she wanted to become a scientist.

A scientist studying stars

Sally Ride studied the stars and planets. She did research at a university. She became a scientist.

In 1977, Sally Ride applied to become an astronaut. Astronauts are people who travel in space. Sally was picked to become an astronaut!

Getting picked was just the start. Next, Sally had to prepare for travel in outer space. She had to learn many different jobs.

Astronauts prepare for space travel

The training was hard. Sally learned how to fly a plane. She learned to jump out of a plane. She learned to use special machines.

Sally had to practice each part of each job in the right sequence. She had to do each part in the right order.

The crew of the *Challenger*, 1983

At last, Sally was ready for one of the most important events in her life. It happened on June 18, 1983.

On that day, Sally and four other
astronauts flew aboard a space shuttle called
the *Challenger*. Sally Ride became the first
American woman to travel in space!

NOTE

NOTE

NOTE

Putting Words to Work

1. Complete this sentence:
   Everything on a spaceship must be done in the
   right **sequence** because _____.

2. What question would you like to ask Sally Ride
   about the **events** in her life?

3. What are two **facts** you learned in this book
   about Sally Ride's life?

4. What topic would you like to learn about by
   doing **research** in a library?

5. **PARTNER ACTIVITY:**   Think of a word you
   learned in the book. Explain its meaning to your
   partner and give an example.

Answer to Word Teaser
research